Deception

The Beautiful Rat

By Jerry Bader

ISBN Paperback: 978-1-988647-59-3

Hard Cover: 978-1-988647-60-9

Ebook: 978-1-988647-61-6

POOR HARRY

Poor Harry

Three Months Earlier

The committee politely listens to my report without much interest. They leaf through some pages as I speak and occasionally nod, but always with a hint of skepticism. Within the first five minutes, I know I'm dead in the water. They let me go on for another fifteen minutes reciting the conclusions and recommendations of six months' research and analysis.

I should have known they were shutting me down as soon as I walked into the room. In addition to the three members of the review committee, there was, Professor Roger Ames, PsyD. They thought I was cracking up. Either that or my report was far too incendiary and imaginative for the bureaucratic brains of the Five Eyes to accept. Best to file it in the trash bin and discredit me as a nutcase.

The Chairman, a priggish, private school twat, delivers the final word without even the pretence of consultation with the other two committee members, "Harry, we do appreciate all the hard work you've done on this report. It is quite comprehensive."

He puts on a smug, self-assured facial contortion that passes for a smile, "Your conclusions and recommendations are nothing if not inventive, but quite frankly a bit fanciful. I'm afraid we'll have to table this document for the time being, but really, quite a nice effort." This arrogant prick is giving me the heave.

"I see..." What can you say, when your boss dismisses six months of deep diving research and analysis. Maybe they'll throw me a bone and give me a field operative to run, just in case. The Chairman pushes his chair back, ready to end the meeting. This is my last chance to get something out of my efforts. "Sir, what about my request for a field agent to follow-up, just in case my conclusions are accurate? What could be the harm?"

The Chairman pauses but doesn't bother to sit back down. His time is important, while mine, isn't.

"I'm afraid we'll have to deny your request, budgetary reasons you understand. The fact is, we think, this assignment has pushed you off the rails a bit. It's not unusual for you cyber boffins to go a little mad when doing these intensive studies. All that time on the laptop, it can drive anyone a little daft, especially someone with a vivid imagination like you."

I try to interject, "But Sir,..."

He raises his hand to shut me up, "Tell you what Harry, take some time off. Take all the time you need to rethink things." He pauses just for a second, "To help you get back on track, we'd like you to meet with Roger..."

Professor Roger Ames stands and approaches me with his hand out. "Hello, Harry. I'm Roger. Nice to meet you."

I instinctively shake his hand. "Gentlemen, I don't need a shrink."

The Chairman smirks. "You know what they say, Harry, denial is a sure sign you need help."

And so the witch floats, proving she is guilty.

HELLO GORGEOUS

Hello Gorgeous

Present Day

You can't escape it. The face is everywhere: on television, on billboards, on posters; plastered on every conceivable surface. It's displayed in bus shelters, store windows, and on those over-sized retail monitors touting the latest got-to-have product, and of course the Internet, always the Internet, the World Wide Weakness of the alienated brain dead.

I wonder if she is even real. Perhaps she's just a hologram, a Photoshop creation, master-minded by some horny millennial doofus working for an ad agency or marketing firm. Whatever or whoever produced and promoted this image, the result is pervasive and sinister; aimed to upend the civilized social order. Something had to be done.

Perhaps it's all in my head, damaged electrical impulses setting off danger signals and paranoia. It's an occupational hazard, reading danger into the most mundane flotsam and jetsam of existence.

I've often thought life is an illusion, and if not an illusion, at least, a malleable truth. Each of us, you included, suffer from the same deception; a movie that we play in our heads for seventy, or eighty, or maybe ninety years if you're lucky.

As directors of our own serial fantasies, we create the heroes and the villains, but always, we are the protagonists, but is it real, or just a mental fiction?

Perhaps we are nothing more than zeroes and ones in a metal box with blinking lights; perhaps it's all a game, a silly fabrication of some greater power, hence our ridiculous clinging to religions that make no sense and cause irreparable harm.

Perhaps it's all a fucking sick joke… my self-absorption is interrupted by the most beautiful creature I've ever seen. She sits down across from me, crosses her long naked legs, and demands: "Buy me a drink, won't you?"

I smile, not so much at the audacity of the demand from the beautiful stranger, but at the notion that I'm a pretty goddamn good casting director for this creation.

She looked familiar, perhaps we met at some party, a quick introduction quickly ignored, then forgotten. No, not this face, this is not a face, men like me could ignore or forget. This is a woman that could melt metal with her smile.

Women like this just don't plop themselves down at my table and demand to be serviced, but then it's my movie, so fuck you, if I want a delicious dish for my femme fatale entrée, that's exactly what I'm going to have.

She reaches into her purse and pulls out a pack of lady cigarettes, she taps the pack with a practised ease, exacts the white poison, and perches it between her pink lips. She doesn't ask for a light, she just waits, widens her electric green eyes, as if to say, 'light me.'

I smile once more at her self-assured cheekiness; I'm determined to match her *chutzpah*. I reach across the table and take the cigarette out of her mouth, "You shouldn't smoke, I don't like kissing smokers."

This time it's her turn to smile, "Bogie and Bergman?" She likes to play the game too, she's my kind of girl, but of course she is, and you know why. I wait a beat and respond, "More Bacall and Bogie."

She leans forward and wantonly eyes the cigarette sitting on the table where I left it. I wished she'd look at me that way. She raises her liquid green orbs to meet my bloodshot circles. She sits back in her chair giving up the desire for a fix. She undoes her coat giving me a better look at her slender well-tendered figure, she sighs, "I know… you don't like kissing smokers."

I wave to a passing waitress, "What would you like?" The stranger's eyes never leave mine, I don't wait for her answer. I order for her, "A screwdriver."

I continue the provocative charade, after all, I play with words for a living; it's my way of competing; I just don't have her physical assets. Like I said before, beautiful women don't fall into my lap every day. I need to make the best of my opportunities, so few come my way.

Her face becomes serious, not hard mind you, just focused, "You report to the Top Floor." It's not a question.

And there it is. Of course, she's not attracted to my middle-age masculine charm. She's in the game, and she wants something. Shit… there goes my fantasy.

She thinks I have influence or at least access; boy is she barking up the wrong tree. Guess she hasn't heard I'm on the shelf with a toe tag labeled 'crazy.'

My mind races, playing successive scenarios over in my head, I'm brought back to life by the bartender changing the channel on the television that hangs over the bar. The ballgame is over and the ten o'clock movie, *The Third Man* is about to start.

The great unwashed at the bar demand the station be changed to something less cerebral and mentally taxing. The only pseudo athletic contest available is darts.

The beautiful stranger's infectious smile brings me back to the issue at hand. She's noticed my mental absence, "Welcome back," she says.

What the hell, I might as well play along, maybe she thinks I'm somebody important; maybe she'll make a pitch that I can parlay into getting my stalled career back on track. Or maybe she'll get me killed or dumped into a warehouse for non-desirables, never to be heard from again. She's playing a dangerous game, and I'm the one in danger.

The drink arrives at the table; she ignores it. She's not in a hurry, she's experienced, she's done this before. It's textbook. She's cast the fly in the water and is trolling for a catch, and I'm the fish.

"Sorry, you must have mistaken me for someone else. I really don't know what you're talking about."

I may be low-level, but I'm not stupid. She doesn't answer immediately. She expected the denial. She eyes the drink but doesn't touch it; perhaps she's afraid of fingerprints, or perhaps she doesn't like vodka. She smiles once more like she can read my mind. "There's no hurry Harry, I can wait… for a while."

Jesus, she knows my name. She gets up from the table, leans over, and kisses me on the mouth. She lingers just for a second and uses her teeth as an exclamation point. She straightens, "Hope I didn't leave a mark?"

"Nothing I can't handle."

"That's good Harry, that's very good, because I do like a close working relationship." She turns and leaves the bar. I don't know whether to laugh or have a panic attack. I look down at her abandoned screwdriver; the cigarette is gone. She's good at her job; It doesn't surprise me.

I need to do something. but what? I can't ignore this, the walls have eyes. The Top Floor gets wind of this and I could end up in a cell. I take the napkin from under her drink and turn it over. I make a quick sketch of her face that is permanently imprinted in my mind. I'll deliver it and a summary of the encounter to Roger in the morning. Or maybe I won't. I have to think. This is either one fucking great movie or the end of my career.

The drunks at the bar decide they've had enough, and darts aren't violent enough for them to watch. Perhaps someone should pitch a new version of darts to the networks where the contestants fire their pointed projectiles at each other instead of a corkboard. The bartender seems to be of the same mind as me. He changes the station back to the movie. What the hell, why waste a good screwdriver and an Orson Welles masterclass. I pick up the orange juice and vodka highball, sit back, and enjoy the performance.

ROGER

Roger

Professor Roger Fitzgerald Ames is your typical middling intelligence service bureaucrat, complete with rumpled tweed, leather shooting patches, brogues, and horn-rimmed spectacles.

He is a pleasant enough chap for the most part; he never raises his voice, never yells or screams, or even demands results. He just questions: *how was your day, anything new, anything you want to tell me?*

Always probing, always searching for something that could endanger the status quo, for that is our real job; not to save the world from Armageddon, but rather, to keep things as they are, so those in charge can carry on doing what they do.

And so I report the incident like a good low-level drudge. I hold back the napkin sketch, not wanting to lay all my cards on the table, at least, not yet. I too could be patient. The service had a history of rotten Philby apples and tainted Profumo politicians with lurid indiscretion and covert mayhem as their stock-in-trade.

I doubted Roger is one of those types, but you never know. His Caspar Milquetoast manner might be a perfect cover for someone willing to indulge in nefarious goings-on. The truth is, I just didn't want to let go of the fantasy.

With my obligation completed, I left Roger's office and headed for my restored antique 1954 MG TF parked across the street from the giant billboard of the omnipresent it-girl that dominates the marketing landscape.

I bought the car from a bankrupt mechanic that spent his last penny resurrecting the beauty. It reminded me of home, a British toy for a half-Brit, half-Canadian nobody, with a distant, safe posting.

It's a good thing I'm independently wealthy, the residue of an ancient Uncle too busy making money to find love and push out dependents. Not that I was a big spender or anything. I managed on my salary, letting my broker pile up the assets or perhaps steal me blind.

The money did provide advantages, like a public school education and a trendy flat filled with Bauhaus furniture and abstract art. We all have our vices, and mine is abstract expressionism.

The money, fancy education, and dual citizenship did get me into the service with a Toronto posting; but without a more aristocratic pedigree or near-genius IQ, I would forever be stalled in my bureaucratic ascent; not unless I'm able to convert my new friend into a winning hand.

As I settle into the driver's seat, she magically reappears. She slips into the passenger side with the grace of an exotic dancer. I was about to say ballerina, but she is far too viscerally sensual for a tutu.

The low slung construction of my ride causes her skirt to ride up just enough for me to catch a glimpse of her naked thigh. She really is beautiful and sexy.

She doesn't bother to adjust her skirt, she just leans over the gear shift and kisses me on the cheek.

"Drive," she demands, and so I do.

"Where to?"

"The Distillery District."

I head south toward the tourist trap, known as the Distillery District, named after the quasi-legal merchants of prohibition vice. The area is now occupied by a series of high-end trendy micro-breweries, art galleries, and shops selling over-priced handcrafted items. I don't ask why The Distillery, I just do what I'm told like a good puppy. I aim to follow her lead, everything will be revealed in due course. As I said, I too could be patient.

"Did you report me to your superiors?"

"Of course.," I say flatly.

"How did you describe me?"

"Attractive, stylish, sexy, and professional."

"So you didn't give Roger the napkin?"

I stop myself from slamming on the brakes and hitting the eject button. How could she know about the napkin, and even more disturbing, how could she know about Roger? I turn to look at her without saying a word. She returns my gaze and smiles, "while you did say I was professional..." she pauses for just a beat like all good actresses, *don't rush the dialogue, let it percolate and simmer, wait for the impact,* "and sexy," she continues. HONK!

My eyes quickly go back to the job at hand, almost too late. The driver of the car next to us angrily mouths something about my mother. She laughs and gives him the finger, not a very spy thing to do, I think. "Of course it is," she says, as she puts her hand on my leg. Christ, she could read my mind, this is bizarre, terrifying, and I admit, a fucking huge turn-on. "Make a right at the lights and park. We'll walk the rest of the way." I obey like an obedient lapdog.

THE NO SHOW

The No Show

We park the car and walk towards the metal overpass, still featuring the Gooderham & Worts word-mark. She pauses under the ancient giant clock and scans the cobblestone path for danger, at least that's what I assume she is doing. Alternatively, she could just be looking for lost loonies.

"There…" she motions us to head towards one of the refurbished retail microbreweries that are a combination pub and working brewery. We enter and find ourselves a place to sit. The bar is clean and tidy with sandblasted walls and rows of spigots fronting a glass panel, behind which is the working brewery. The place is the perfect location for trendy twenty-somethings to take their dates, or for a couple of spooks to make contact.

"Before this goes any further, I need to know who you work for? Lie to me and I'll *fuck'n* shoot you where you sit."

I am being overly dramatic, but I need to make a point. She thinks for a second not quite sure how to take my feeble Bond imitation. She smiles, "Do you carry a gun, Harry?"

"No…" I figure why lie? What's good for the goose is good for the gander. We need to be straight with one another if this relationship is going to work, besides, she knows I'm bluffing; she can read my fucking mind. She knows what I'm going to say before I say it.

"Shall we order then?"

"I don't drink beer."

"I guess this isn't a very good place for a first date."

"Is that what this is?"

She reaches across the table and takes the coaster I've been playing with, out of my hand. She takes my hand in hers, "No this isn't."

I get up from the table forcing her to release my hand, "I'm leaving. You can call a cab or one of those trendy car services. I'm tired of this game."

"Sit down for god's sake." That's twice she's called my bluff. I wouldn't want to play poker with this girl even if I knew how.

"Harry, please sit down. You know better than to call attention to us." I sit. "You really are sweet, you know."

I respond without humour, "Yah… like a good puppy."

A waitress interrupts our conversation, "What can I get you?"

"I don't drink beer."

She looks at me like I'm crazy. "Well, I guess you're in the perfect place."

"No need to be sarcastic, we're waiting for a friend."

"Oh.." she says, "WE'LL comeback when they arrive." She turns and heads for a table of tourists.

"Calm yourself, Harry, I'll tell you what you want to know."

"Okay… let's have it."

"I kinda work for the same people you do. Different department of course."

"Which department would that be?"

"Well it's not exactly a department, it's more of a task force, kinda what the cops call Internal Affairs."

"You're investigating me?"

"Don't be silly Harry, You're not important enough to investigate."

"Thanks, you sure know how to pump up a guy's ego." What the hell was I saying? I was actually complaining about not being a security threat.

She laughs. "You are adorable, Harry, my very own sad little puppy."

"Fuck you." The words come out of my mouth without me realizing I said them out loud.

She laughs, "All in good time Harry, all in good time."

If my male ego was bruised, she deftly manages to turn it around. She could see my rusting synapses trying to ponder the real meaning of her response. She doesn't allow me to dwell on it, "The target is someone higher up the food chain."

"Roger?"

"I doubt it, but you never know. It's a good thing you didn't give him the napkin. You have good instincts."

I'm starting to feel better about myself. She knows just what to tell me so I'll go along. "What exactly are we doing here?"

"We're supposed to meet up with an American from their Consulate, but he's a no-show. He might be the guy that contacted our rat."

"Is he a double?"

"Maybe."

"So why would he help us put his contact's neck in a noose?"

"He probably doesn't see it that way. I mean, he could be a full-fledged SVR asset, but more likely he just thinks he's doing his job. The spy business is murky at the best of times. He probably figured it's the Brits, what real harm could it do, and if he picked up a little extra spending money, all the better."

"Isn't that good for our side?"

"It would be, if our boy reported it, which he didn't. The Americans aren't sure if this guy is the rat, so they want us to find our Benedict Arnold and work backward to see who it is and how deep this operation goes." I shake my head in disbelief, "Is there really someone that stupid working for us? Haven't we had enough Philbys for several lifetimes?"

"You'd be surprised. The disgruntled, politically naive and just plain greedy surround us like a vice."

"So the Americans are demanding we find the rats and stem the flow of information."

"You know how these things start. The American figures he can put one in his column and make a little fuck-you-cash for his retirement. The next time he needs a favour, he's got one hell of an IOU in the bank. The trouble is, our boy had another agenda."

"So Langley doesn't appreciate ad-libbing."

"Fuck no," she says. "But guys on the sharp end of the stick think differently. They know things aren't black and white. Sometimes you have to work with people no matter what side of the wall they report to. You don't get if you don't give."

"I didn't think the Americans worked that way."

"Officially they don't, but as I said, the bureau-crats and politicians aren't on the front lines."

"So what happened to your boy?"

"I don't know, we better go check it out." She gets up to leave.

I hesitate, "One more thing..."

"What's that?"

"Your name? What do I call you?" She thinks for a second before replying, "Harriet, you can call me Harriet."

"You had to think about it?"

"Don't be so cynical Harry. It's a perfectly good name. Harry and Harriet, we wouldn't even have to change the monogram on the towels."

THE AMERICAN

The American

The contact's name is Chester MacDonald. He lives in a rented house just west of Avenue Road, north of Eglinton. It's a quiet neighbourhood with homes that range from small, comfy, post-WWII centre-halls to more recent monster renovations, that flout their opulence like Gordon Gekko snapping his suspenders. MacDonald's residence is the former.

I knock on the front door. No answer. "Try the bell," she commands, but still no answer. "Let's try the back."

We take the narrow cement slab path to the backyard, climb the worn wooden-porch steps and tap on the window that tops the back door. Still no response. "What do we do now? Pick the lock?"

She looks at me, "You know how to pick a lock, Harry?" My face goes red.

"Skipped that day in spy school, did we?" she says as she scans the porch. She spots a forgotten shovel in the corner. She picks it up and jabs the handle through the glass windowpane. She looks at me, "Use your imagination Harry, adapt."

I reach through the broken window, cutting my hand in the process, "Fuck!" I grab a hankie from my pocket to squelch the flow of blood.

She looks at me with what I assume is pity, "Be careful what you touch. I'll kiss it better later."

We enter the house through the kitchen that backs onto the porch. It's quiet, nobody's home. "He's probably at the Consulate," she says.

We go through the small kitchen to the equally tiny dining room. The living room isn't much bigger. It's the kind of place real estate agents call 'cozy,' claustrophobic is more appropriate.

There are no toys, no knick-knacks, no family photos, and not much in the way of furniture. The place is in dire need of some expert staging.

Harriet goes upstairs to check the bedrooms while I look for a den. There's a door that leads to a room across from the living room. It's Chester's office. It's bigger than I expected and it looks well-used. In fact, it looks like it's the only room in the house that shows any signs of human habitation.

There's a couch with a pillow and blankets, the room must have served as his bedroom. The coffee table is strewn with several pizza boxes with stale leftover remains of crust slowly growing hair.

I hear Harriet's voice from behind me, "I don't understand people who order pizza and don't eat the crust." I turn to look at her, "I know Harry, you were thinking the exact same thing. We're like two peas in a pod." I start to say something but she points, "I think we found our boy."

I turn to look. Sure enough, the late Chester MacDonald is head down on his desk as if he's sleeping, a long endless nap evidenced by the dried blood that has found its resting place like Chester, atop the front page of The Toronto Star.

The remains of a shattered e-cig litter the newspaper. Lifting Chester's head reveals a pointed metal fragment from the electronic device sticking deep into his forehead. "That's one way to stop smoking," she says. Her tone is more than a little cavalier for someone whose contact was murdered by a smoking cessation device.

"Must have been one of those off-market batteries. They have a habit of going bang."

"You think it was an accident?" she says.

"Don't you?" She ignores the question but asks, "What's he pointing to?" I hadn't noticed that his middle finger is pointing to a small article at the bottom of the page, just under one of those ads featuring the ever-present advertising it-girl. The headline is partly covered in blood, but it's still readable: **"Island Residents Evicted, Foreign Corp Buys Island Airport"**

"Maybe this Island business has something to do with his faulty e-cig battery."

"That stuff is way over my pay-grade. All I know is what I read in the paper. Come to think of it, Roger did have me put together some background on the Island: how many people, the number of buildings, square footage… that sort of thing. It seemed kind of strange at the time; nothing more than busywork. Why would he give a damn about some local real estate?"

"Think airport Harry… a quiet, isolated location, nowhere near Langley, where our American pals can come and go without notice. All you have to do is get rid of the locals and drop in a bunch of Mormon types. Bingo, the CIA boys can go where they want, when they want, and the Comrades don't even notice."

FOREIGN CORP BUYS ISLAND AIRPORT

"Why would the Canadians go for that?"

"Who knows, tit-for-tat. Maybe it's a joint operation, maybe the Yanks finally gave up the softwood tariff bullshit. It doesn't matter. What matters is why we weren't in on the deal."

"So our boys must have got their noses out of joint. The Americans and Canadians are planning something big, leaving us in the dark. Chester contacts one of our guys figuring why shouldn't his MI6 pals know; maybe he can put together a nice IOU that he can cash in later. Not to mention some real dough. The next thing you know, we're picking e-cig fragments out of Chester's cerebral cortex."

"Could be Harry. Nobody likes a tattletale."

"I thought we were all on the same side?"

"Spying is a dangerous business, Harry. One wrong move and you won't have to buy any more Nicorette. So we better watch our asses from now on."

"Or stop using battery-powered devices."

THE INTERROGATION

The Interrogation

They knock on my door at six o'clock in the morning, Metro cops. All they say is they want to talk to me downtown and no I couldn't take my car; they'd drive, a kind of Uber for criminals, but I wasn't a criminal was I? What's a little break-and-enter when national security is on the line, but I guess it depends on whose national interests are being protected.

They parked under the billboard of the ever-present advertising queen and proceeded to stuff me in the back of one of their black and whites; the kind with a screen protecting the driver just in case I tried a Bourne-style escape.

We drive directly to 22 Division where I'm unceremoniously shoved into a holding cell to wait for what I expected to be a brown-shirted interrogator complete with a bag full of needles and a year's supply of Sodium Pentothal. I'm probably over-reacting again; I hope.

They come for me after what seems like an eternity; I couldn't tell exactly because they took my watch, belt, and wallet. I understood the belt, just in case I wanted to hang myself for smashing some guys window, but I didn't get taking my wallet. Perhaps they were afraid I might buy my way out of jail by offering the drunk in the next cell a twenty, or more likely, they were worried I might commit suicide by American Express Card. The picture in my mind wasn't pretty. I do have an active imagination.

When they came, they took me through what I assumed was the detective's squad room. Most of them seemed to be drinking coffee or banging away on their computers, probably video games, since according to the paper, the criminal conviction rates were less than impressive. One crack Dick Tracy was reading the morning tabloid with the face of the omnipresent it-girl staring back at me as if to say everything will be alright.

I spotted Harriet sitting beside Roger on a metal bench in the waiting area. Roger half waved with his Graf von Faber-Castell pen, assuring me he was there to see I wasn't water-boarded; Harriet's hand went to her lips with one finger notifying me to keep my fucking mouth shut.

They put me in a small putrid pale green room with buzzing fluorescents that blinked like they were in desperate need of some remedial medication. They let me sit there on a hard metal chair with a cracked vinyl seat cushion for quite some time. I absentmindedly picked away at the polyester filler while trying to figure out whether the stains on the wall formed an image of Guy Burgess or Anthony Blunt.

I tend toward a pretty active case of benign Pareidolia; hopefully not extending into the more troubling realm of Apophenia; To date, I haven't started wearing a tinfoil hat, at least, not that I am aware.

Two beefy *bulvuns* enter to verbally slap me around. They identify themselves, but their names go in one ear and out the other. I'm too busy deciding if the presumed bloodstain on the wall looks more like Burgess or Blunt. In my mind, I identify the taller cop as Tom and the short bald one as Dick. It seems appropriate since I am Harry, and like the similarly named Stalag Luft III tunnels, escape is unlikely.

Tom: "Want to tell us why you broke into Chester MacDonald's house?"

"Who says I broke into someone's house?"

Dick: "We do."

I turned from Tom to look at Dick. I named him appropriately.

Tom: "Your blood was on some broken glass found in his kitchen."

I turn my head back to Tom, "You don't say?"

Dick: "Yah, we do say!"

I'm starting to get a stiff neck from ping-ponging back and forth. I decide to just ignore Dick, and concentrate on Tom. "You know I really don't have any memory of breaking anybody's window, at least not since I was a kid."

Dick: "Stop fucking around and give us what we want."

I continued to ignore the fat slob. I look up at Tom, "You really should tell your partner to tuck in his shirt. He looks rather unkempt. Such sartorial disregard might lead serious criminals, ones that do a trifle more than break a window, to think a sloppy attire equals a sloppy mind; one easily deceived with obfuscation and prevarication."

The two cops look at one another not sure if they should laugh or punch me in the face. I don't give them a chance to ponder their decision.

"So… were any of Mr. MacDonald's prized possessions missing, or perhaps a skeleton fell out of one of his closets." I hope my smart-ass routine will make me look innocent, which technically I am since it was Harriet who broke the window.

"Gee Officer Krupke, I'm innocent, really I am." If they keep questioning me much longer I might have to do the whole *West Side Story* routine."

Dick: "This English muffin is nuts."

"Technically, I'm only half an English muffin, the other half is Canadian." I don't wait for a reply, "So are you going to arrest me for breaking Mr. MacDonald's window or his murder." The last part just slipped out. Oops, Harriet won't be pleased.

Tom: "What makes you think MacDonald was murdered?"

Maybe I'll have to do a little tap dancing after all. "Oh I don't know, maybe having the Gestapo knock on my door at six in the morning might signal I'm being accused of something more serious than a broken pane of glass."

Tom: "You know where MacDonald is?"

"Excuse me?"

Dick: "What are you deaf, as well as dumb?"

"You didn't see MacDonald?"

Tom: "We spoke to his boss at the consulate. He's been reassigned to Finland."

What happened to the body? What the fuck is going on? All these guys got is some broken glass.

Dick: "I think we should hang on to this prick for a few days. Maybe he'll be more willing to talk after he spends a few nights in lockup with some of our fair city's less desirable citizens."

"Well boys, it's been a pleasure, but I'm afraid broken windows aren't a capital offence, besides I didn't want to break it to you earlier because, well, talking to you is a real pleasure, but I do have diplomatic immunity since I work for the British Government. So in the words of someone famous, *fuck-off and let me go*."

After some further verbal jousting, they give me back my watch, belt, and wallet. I check to see if my American Express Card is still where it's supposed to be. It is.

Harriet and Roger are no longer parked on the metal bench. I guess my friends at the police station are somewhat offended by my lack of cooperation because I have to take the bus back to my condo, which is fine. It gives me time to think about what happened to Chester and his exploding e-cig. And, what exactly were the Americans and Canadians doing on Toronto Island?

MOVIE TIME

Movie Time

I arrive back at the condo in the late afternoon. I realize I need to pee; it had been a long day without relief and my interrogators were not inclined to offer the use of their facilities.

As I stand waiting for my nervous middle-aged prostate to relax, I wonder why all new movies must have a scene with some guy peeing. Bogey never had to pee. It seems decidedly unnecessary, and it rarely moves the plot forward, but this is my movie and if the powers that be want a pee scene... well fuck it, I'll give it to them.

When I finally finish what I had to do, I go into the living room and turn on the television. The flat-screen springs to life with my go-to station replaying *The Third Man*. Joseph Cotton is still trying to find who killed his pal, Orson Welles.

I stand staring at the screen practically mouthing the words. I've seen the movie so many times I know the dialogue off by heart. To my mind, it's the best of Noir.

The harpsichord starts its haunting theme while a bunch of guys in hats chase Joseph Cotton up a winding staircase. I stand transfixed. Cotton suddenly disappears and the ubiquitous pitch-girl takes his place hawking her latest must-have potion; a concoction that will turn every ugly ducking into a human aphrodisiac.

I decide I'm in desperate need of a caffeine transfusion. I go into the kitchen to make myself my daily ration of coffee. I'd just purchased one of those new-fangled contraptions that only uses proprietary pods with exotic foreign names and descriptive labels that one would normally expect to find describing vintage wines. The noise from the gizmo drowns out the television. With my freshly brewed cup of over-priced java in hand, I re-enter the living room.

As I do, I see the back of a beautiful woman's head popping up from the other side of the couch facing the TV. I know she's beautiful because I'd recognize those luscious tresses anywhere: it's Harriet. I start to speak but she raises her hand, "Listen, Harry, this is the best part. I love this part."

Orson Welles smirks at his pal, Cotton, while he delivers one of cinema's most famous lines, *"In Italy for thirty years under the Borgias, they had warfare, terror, murder, and bloodshed. They produced, Michaelangelo, da Vinci, and the Renaissance. In Switzerland, they had brotherly love, five hundred years of democracy and peace, and what did they produce? The cuckoo clock."*

I had to admit, I love that scene too, but there are more pressing issues at hand. "How did you get in? There's a doorman, and; a lock on the door."

"Don't be silly Harry. Doormen are *easy pickins* for a pretty lady, and I am, I think, a very pretty lady..."

She pauses using her best Bergman timing. She's a master of cadence and subtext. "You agree I'm pretty, don't you Harry?" She doesn't wait for my answer, mostly because she knows what I think before I think it.

She turns her body so her head faces me. She rests her chin on her arm that's settled on the back of the tuxedo style Parsons couch. "You see Harry, my dear, I didn't miss that day in spy school."

"You picked the lock?"

"Well, what did you think? I transported myself magically through the door."

"I don't know. It wouldn't surprise me." It is a weak comeback, but I'm doing the best I can under the circumstances. My brain finally switches gears. "What's a matter? Couldn't find a shovel"

She sighs a sensual sigh feigning exasperation with my naivety. "Poor Harry... such a bad day. All stressed out because of a little problem with the police."

"What happened to Chester's body?"

"I looked after it."

"You looked after it," I repeated unnecessarily.

"Yes, Harry my dear. No need to be redundant."

"While I sure wouldn't want to be fucking redundant."

"You serve a purpose," she says.

"I see."

"Don't you think a thank you is in order, perhaps a kiss would be a just reward."

"You looked after it?" I repeated, unsure of exactly what the implications of that fact entailed. I took a seat on a matching Parsons chair as far away from Harriet as possible. I took a sip of coffee to steady my nerves. I'm starting to comprehend what it all meant.

"You work for the Americans."

She smiles her delicious smile while patting the cushion beside her, urging me to join her on the couch. I resist. "Come on Harry, play nice, I did save your ass."

"You said you worked for us."

"I said I worked for a task force. A small but important distinction."

"Not so small if you ask me."

"We're still friends, aren't we, Harry?"

"You killed Chester and set me up. You fucking know how to pick a lock but you chose to break the window instead, hoping I'd cut myself leaving evidence."

"My bad Harry, but I had to know."

"Know what?"

"Whether we could trust you. You proved yourself with Tom and Dick."

"Get out!"

She doesn't move.

"You know I have to report this to Roger."

"But Roger, the dear man, has been in on this from the start. He's the one that put me onto you."

"Jesus Christ... You and Roger killed Chester because he went rogue and set me up for the murder. So why clean up; why get me off the hook?"

"It was decided you could be of more use, and besides the body can reappear anytime we want. And you're still number one on Tom and Dick's hit list."

"Who told the cops Chester went to Finland?"

"I did... Now, why don't you make me one of those fancy coffees and relax? We can talk about these paintings of yours, and what you see in them."

I did what she wanted. I made the coffee, and we settled in on the couch talking abstract expressionism. She seemed rather fascinated by my ability to see faces in the oil and pigment; elements that are neither intended nor there. I explained my Pareidolia away as a combination of the frustration of an amateur painter and an overactive imagination.

"Are you sure it's not a case of Apophenia? Perhaps you should see someone other than Roger. I wouldn't want to be seen driving around in your toy car with you wearing a tinfoil hat."

God this woman is scary. Perhaps she practises Vulcan mind-meld techniques along with her ability to pick locks and appear as if out of thin air.

"Harry my dear, I do seem to be developing a severe headache. Could you get me some tablets and water?"

Her request brought me back to earth. I go into the master bedroom en suite where I keep my rather copious supply of headache meds and return with two Extra Strength Tylenol and a glass of water. She's gone.

Her fancy coffee sits on the glass coffee table untouched. Beside it is a manila file folder with a yellow Post-It note stuck to the top. Printed neatly in block letters: MEMO FOUND AT CHESTER'S.

I realized then that my head is throbbing in a syncopated rhythm of pain. How did she know? "Fascinating." Perhaps she really is Mr. Spock in drag.

I took the pills and flipped open the file folder using the tip of my Pilot Vanishing Point pen. She set me up once with the broken window, I wasn't going to fall for the same trick twice.

There is only one sheet of yellow foolscap paper in the file. It's a list of six names under the head-line: *The Sister Project*. I scan the names but only recognized two: C. MacDonald and R. F. Ames.

OH, ROGER, WHAT HAVE YOU DONE?

Oh, Roger, What Have You Done?

As I head for a scheduled meeting with Roger, I question, exactly how much I should tell him? Harriet claims she's working with him on this secret task-force charged with finding a Russian mole, but what if Roger and Harriet are both SVR assets and Chester and I are being set up as the patsies? If Roger isn't the mole, and he finds out I've been up close and personal with Harriet, and she turns out to be the rat, then it's cell time for me. If Roger and Harriet are both double agents, then I'm royally screwed, probably dead.

Britain couldn't afford another Kim Philby episode, especially with the Brexit nonsense still causing major problems.

Is the list left by Harriet the names of possible sleeper agents, or is it a list of task force members? In either case, is Harriet's name on it?

The only name on the list that starts with an H is H. K. Krysa, and who knew if Harriet is even her real name.

The other names on the list were C. MacDonald, R. F. Ames, T. Harrison, W. J. Gordon, and W. T Marsh.

Was Chester killed because he leaked information on a joint USA-Canadian covert operation to the British or because the guy he leaked it to is a Russian asset?

If Chester was just an innocent fool why kill him when he could be an ongoing source of information? Once you play footsie with the enemy, they got you by the balls.

Was there really a task force? Who does Harriet actually work for and did Roger and Harriet kill Chester to protect Roger's cover or to eliminate a suspected Russian agent? What did it all mean? And why the hell did Harriet bring me into this mess, unless I was being set up to take the fall? I had a sinking feeling this was not going to end well for me.

I knock on Roger's door. "Come in dear boy, come in."

He places some papers he was reading in the bottom drawer of his desk, making an extravagant show of locking the papers away in an obvious attempt to impress me with their importance. After all, unimportant people don't have secret papers.

Perhaps it's an attempt to present himself as a pompous poser showing off to a subordinate in a display of puffery when in fact it's an attempt at misdirection: act overly important, signalling that in fact, you're a nobody. It is all very confusing. Was my combined Paranoia and Pareidolia getting out of hand? Was I seeing things that weren't really there? No! This is not my imagination, something is fishy, and I am going to get to the bottom of it, no matter, who got hurt.

"Tell me dear boy, have the headaches improved any, less frequent, less severe?"

"Haven't had a headache in a couple of weeks," I lied.

"Well done my son, well done. That's what I like to hear. Getting control of those emotions."

The meeting went on with Roger doing his usual psychobabble probing with me lobbing back every query with an equally unintelligible response. I wasn't sure what these meetings were about, or what purpose they served. In fact, I have no idea what earthly service I provide to the Crown. All I do all day is sift through newspapers and Internet sites looking for something, but I never know what that something is. If I ask, the answer is always the same, "You'll know when you see it, dear boy, you'll know."

The whole thing seemed stupid, but we are talking about the government. One hopes that there is a point to the whole exercise. At least the business with Harriet provides some excitement and the company of a beautiful woman. On the downside, I could get labeled a spy and spend the rest of my days in a dungeon at some foreign black site having electrical wires attached to my testicles.

MY MCQUEEN MOMENT

My McQueen Moment

Steve McQueen had his Mustang, I got my MG. I had a similar Mustang model at one time and I have to tell you; I hated that car. You couldn't see out the back worth a shit because the rear window was pitched at far too severe an angle and the side windows in the back, didn't roll down.

I remember when the car was new, one of my friends had broken up with his girlfriend, so to cheer him up, I figured me and some pals would take him out for a night on the town. We spent the evening drinking and flirting with the local talent, but my friend was too upset to close the deal. We ended up at the No. 7 Chinese Restaurant that was located up a rickety flight of stairs over a laundry that I'm sure was a front for some sort of gambling operation. As you climbed the stairs, you could hear the Mah Jong tiles clicking, accompanied by Cantonese exclamations of POK GAAI! that I later found out translates to "fall in the street" but means "drop dead."

The food at No. 7 is psychedelic in palette and pungent in aroma. My friend filled himself with vast quantities of undetermined red, orange, and yellow delicacies. On the way out he stood unsteady at the top of the stairs. His face matched a shade of green that would have made a perfect complement to the rainbow concoctions he had just consumed. He then proceeded to vomit.

I still remember catching him before he fell forward joining the regurgitated mess as it slowly made its way down each step like the lumpy flow of the Yangtze River.

We sidestepped the colourful ooze and made our way to my car. We figured it was safe to take my friend home since it was unlikely there was anything left in his stomach, evidenced by the copious amounts of fried shrimp and lemon chicken that made its way down the steps of No. 7. Of course, we were wrong.

Driving back to my friend's place he decided he had to throw-up one more time. My other friends frantically tried to locate the handle to roll down the back window so he could get some air, or at least make sure my new car continued to exude that wonderful new car smell, but Ford had a better idea: the back windows did not roll down. After that incident, I got rid of that piece of shit as soon as possible. God, I hated that car.

All of this flashes through my head like a porn movie junkie fast-forwarding to the good parts as I make my way down Woodbine Avenue to the

Don Valley Parkway. The incident seemed to be triggered by a brief glimpse of a green Mustang muscling in behind a silver Honda two cars back. My youthful memories change channels with visions of a super cool, turtlenecked Steve McQueen chasing a Dodge Charger around the streets of San Francisco.

I hit the gas as I enter the on-ramp to the Don Valley. If you don't get up to speed fast on this downhill thrill ride from the top of the city to the bottom, you'll be run over by oncoming exurbanites eager to partake of the more exotic downtown pleasures.

I pull onto the Parkway almost taking out a Volkswagen Bug and Ford Escape. I glance in my rearview to see if any of the citizens I scared are threatening revenge. They aren't, but they also aren't too thrilled with the Mustang that recklessly followed my lead.

Is my new muscle car buddy just a jerk or does he want to play? I hit the accelerator and my little MG responds like a real sports car, not one of those fancy American imitation wannabes. You can add bucket seats to anything and call it a sports model, but that doesn't make it a sports car.

Travelling down the Don Valley is like being shot out of a cannon. Even regular daily commuters and little old ladies looking for downtown bargains become crazed maniacs barreling down the Don.

I weave in and out of traffic like Stirling Moss taking on the Nürburgring. My muscle car mate follows suit. He does want to play. Both of us dart in and out of lanes to the sounds of irate civilians leaning heavily on their horns and brakes.

I take the cutoff at Rosedale Valley Road figuring the muscle car madman is just a jerk and will continue downtown, but he doesn't. He follows me onto Rosedale Valley. Despite the fact this twisting scenic connector is in the heart of the city, you'd swear you were in the country surrounded by age-old trees and greenery.

Perhaps this is a mistake. Maybe my Mustang mate is a better driver than I am, I could end up wrapped around a Canadian Maple. I doubt if too many people would raise a glass to dear old Harry. Maybe Harriet and Roger might share a glass or two, but car aficionados would surely hold a *shiva* for my little MG.

My British sports coupe and the American poser twist and turn in a desperate vehicle tango. The speed limit is fifty kilometres but we are both hitting triple digits taking corners on two wheels. We hit a straightaway, and the duel is on. He easily pulls up beside me but before he could force me off the road, I down-shift with a heel-and-toe technique and brace for the worst.

The MG groans but slows and my opponent flies by like an F15. He slams on his brakes while I hit the accelerator one more time. I double clutch to get up to speed. I pass him with a smirk and a French Connection subway scene wave.

The Mustang attempts to recover but I've gained the advantage. I pay no attention to the annoying stop signs the city fathers have strategically placed to annoy me. I turn onto Bloor Street and lose my pal in the heavy traffic. I hear a loud crash from behind. A quick look in the rear mirror and I smile. A t-boned late-model green Mustang rests-in-peace in the middle of midtown Toronto.

MR. BOWLEY

Mr. Bowley

Who can I trust? What's really going on? How can I protect myself? Whose side is Harriet actually on? And what about Roger, is he friend or foe?

I have the sinking feeling that I am being played for a fool. Harriet may be nothing more than a sophisticated honey trap, so obvious that paranoids like me hesitate to take the facts at face value. She came right out and admitted she set me up, almost bragged about it, but with a smile and offhandedness that implied, '*just kidding lover.*' But despite the alluring glint in her eye, the admission was a definite threat, '*play along or you'll get screwed.*'

Who would want to make me a patsy and for what reason? It could be anybody: the Americans, the Canadians, the Russians... maybe even my own people. So much for Queen and country. I can just hear those Vauxhall Cross assholes in their three-piece Savile Row made-to-measures saying, "*well old boy, he's a nice chap, but someone has to take the fall, and besides he's only half British, not really one of us.*"

I was in a box and I had to find a way out. The only real clue I had, to what was going on, was the file Harriet left for me, *The Sister Project*. Maybe it's the bread crumb I'm supposed to follow that will put me in a cell, or maybe it's just a false trail, a misdirection, leading me away from what's really going on. Was the Toronto Island business just another false lead?

I found myself in what the locals call The Village, a trendy shopping and art gallery area that I know well from my excursions into the realm of abstract expressionism.

I find a rare parking spot on Hazelton Lanes only a half a block from my destination, The Bowley Gallery, owned and operated by Andrew Bowley. Commander Bowley, he preferred to be addressed as Mister, is an old Cold War SIS boffin specializing in cloak-and-dagger relationships fostered under the cover of an international art dealer par excellence.

He is as close to a personal and professional mentor as I have. Officially he's retired, and no longer has any association with the men that occupy the upper floors of Vauxhall Cross. But as anyone who has ever been in the spy business knows, once you're in, you're in for life.

Whether my supposed accidental initial meeting with Mr. Bowley was in fact by chance, or secretly arranged, is anyone's guess, I'll leave that to your vivid imagination to figure out. The fact is, Mr. Bowley taught me everything I know about abstract art, and how to survive the Machiavellian bureaucratic trenches of the Secret Intelligence Service.

I enter the gallery and I'm greeted by a pretty receptionist who recognizes me from my frequent visits and the substantial cheques left behind.

"Is Mr. Bowley in?"

The woman looks at me strangely. "You ask that every time you come in. You know where he is, he's in the Park."

"Yes, of course, he is."

"Would you like to see some of the new additions? They're quite exciting, and they're right up your alley."

"Ah… not right now, maybe next time, but thank you for thinking of me."

I leave the gallery and head for Park Lane Cemetery around the corner. I stop and purchase two English teas from one of those trendy new tea shops that think they'll catch-on like the ever-present coffee franchises that appear on every block. It's wishful thinking if you ask me, coffee drinkers and tea drinkers are like dog lovers and cat people, they are just not the same in taste or habit.

As I enter the elaborate iron gate entrance I spot Bowley sitting on a park bench. He's visiting his late wife. I sit down beside him and offer the tea.

"Crackerjack, my son. How nice of you to visit."

He always called me Crackerjack, a nickname he reserved for his favorites. He places the tea beside him.

"It's not real tea you know? Not like the tea back home."

"Yes, Sir, I know. I'm afraid I've caught the local coffee addiction."

"It's a nice gesture anyway my son."

Bowley is an elegant eighty-something with wispy white hair, slim physique, and military bearing. He is every bit the English gentleman. He must have been quite the prize for Mrs. Bowley back in the day.

I present him with my conundrum as I sip my tea and he ignores his. He listens quietly, occasionally rubbing his chin as if ruminating on my dilemma, or perhaps forcing himself to stay awake. When I finish he sits for a moment and ponders the issue at hand.

"Well, Crackerjack, there is no point in *losing the plot*." I smile at the old fashion British expression meaning I shouldn't become unhinged. "Let me see that list."

I hand the old man the list. "*The Sister Project,* very interesting, very interesting indeed,"

"You know what it is Sir?"

"I hear things you know, some I should, and some I shouldn't. Occasionally old friends like you come by for a chat, but not so much anymore. Still, I hear things from *gormless muppets*. None of them ever bought any paintings like you. Most of them were boring chaps with no appreciation for the abstract, for the non-linear aspects of a thing. You're special my boy. You appreciate the non-representational aspects of life, the subtext hidden beneath mundane facades. I'm not ashamed to say you were always my favorite.

When these visitors say things they aren't supposed to say, I make note of it. I guess they figure, what's the harm. But I still have a few working brain cells and all the old files and even some newer ones are filed away somewhere safe. Sort of an insurance policy kind of thing."

I wasn't sure if he was advising me to do the same, or if he was just lost in distant memories of operations gone wrong.

"Sir... *The Sister Project*?"

"You know about the Chapman business of course?"

"Yes Sir... everyone knows about her. She ran the Illegals Program."

"The Yanks just don't get it. Everything with them is short-term, instant results, instant gratification, quick promotion up the covert ladder. The Russians and the Chinese play the long game. They understand, sometimes things work, and sometimes they don't. But just because some operation doesn't succeed the first time, doesn't mean that it won't work the next time with a few tweaks. My guess, *The Sister Project* is the Illegals reinvented."

"You mean this is a list of sleeper agents?"

"That's what I'm saying my boy, but of course, I could be wrong. It's happened before, and I am an old fool they've put out to pasture."

"So, Chester MacDonald and Roger Ames, along with these other four people are Russian sleeper agents."

"Well I can't say definitively, but there is one very interesting name on the list."

"Which one?"

"Seems like you've let your Russian slide a little, my boy."

"I know a few things Sir: how to swear, find the bathroom, and order vodka."

"Yes, all the essentials." He pauses to catch his breath, "H. K. Krysa, that's the name I'd be interested in learning more about."

"Why that name?"

"*Krasivaya Krysa*, (*Красивая Крыса*), the *Beautiful Rat,* that's what it means. Back in the day, it used to be a code name for the one in charge of a

covert operation like the Illegals. This woman
that keeps popping up everywhere, what did you
say her name is?"

"Harriet."

"Yes, Harriet… maybe she's H. K. Krysa."

This is not good news. We talk a little longer, and
I leave. As I cross the street on the way back to
my car, I notice a video playing in the window of
a high-priced hair salon. It features the ubiquitous advertising beauty shaking her glorious
coiffed mane demonstrating the latest Sassoon
style du jour. When I get back to my car, Harriet
is waiting for me, leaning on my fender like she's
posing for some high fashion glossy.

"Harry my love, have a nice chat with the Commander?"

THE DOUBTING TOMMY

The Doubting Tommy

Earlier that same day Internet hacker Tommy Harrison, right-wing conservative political bag-man, Walter T. Marsh, and crackpot conspiracy theory radio host and blogger Wade J. Gordon meet for brunch.

Tommy Harrison is twenty-five and looks twelve; March is fifty and looks seventy, and Gordon is what he is, a middle-aged frustrated prick, who always thinks he's the smartest guy in the room, when in fact he's just a loud-mouth jerk.

The meeting isn't going as planned. Marsh is pissed off but remains professionally calm; Gordon is furious and doesn't bother to conceal it; Harrison is scared.

Marsh pushes a thick manila envelope across the table in Harrison's direction, "Look, Tommy, here's the rest of the money and the list of websites. You know what needs to be done." Tommy looks at the envelope but doesn't touch it.

Gordon can't contain his emotions, a character flaw that endears him to the Neanderthal, white trash racists, and flyover nincompoop listeners and readers that don't believe in government unless it's a subsidy that prolongs their narrow-minded parochial existence. "Do what you're told, kid! Or else!"

"Listen, fellows," says Tommy, "this isn't right. The stuff you're putting out is total bullshit. It's one thing to try to sway public opinion with facts and argument; it's totally another to fix an election. Besides, look at the shit storm it created the last time it was done. This time they'll be on the lookout. It's far too dangerous. And I'm not going to jail for you two clowns, no matter how much dough you push in my direction."

Marsh reaches across the table in an attempt to grab Tommy by the throat, but Gordon intervenes. "For Christ's sake Wade, calm down. The kid's just a little skittish. He'll come through for us. He really doesn't have a choice, he's already been paid half, and from what I understand that money is gone, so he can't pay it back. He has no choice. Right, Tommy?"

"Fuck the both of you!" Tommy gets up and heads for the front counter to pay his bill. He leaves Marsh's envelope on the table. Gordon is apoplectic. He starts to go after Tommy but Marsh stops him. "Sit the fuck down."

Marsh takes out his cell phone and dials a number. "It's as we feared. He's resigned. He's just about to leave. His car is parked across the street from the restaurant... Okay, but we'll need a replacement."

Tommy pays his bill and leaves the coffee shop. He takes out his cell phone and dials a number as he starts to run across the busy downtown intersection.

An old, red German sports car darts out of an alley directly opposite the coffee shop. Tommy doesn't see the coupe until it makes contact, propelling him through the window of the dry cleaner located next to the restaurant.

Marsh and Gordon pay their bill and leave. Tommy Harrison is dead and Harry's list is getting shorter.

Marsh turns to Gordon, "We better watch our asses. One wrong move and we'll be the next ones to go."

Gordon grunts, "Don't be such a chicken-shit. All you do is raise money and make telephone calls. I'm the one on the front lines every day."

Marsh grabs Gordon by the shoulder, turning him around so they're face-to-face. "Don't be stupid Wade. A loud mouth won't protect you from these fuckers."

HARRIET COMES CLEAN?

Harriet Comes Clean?

I drove for what seemed quite some time before Harriet spoke. "Well Harry, I guess it's time to come clean."

I'm not sure Harriet is capable of telling the truth, at least not the whole truth. but breadcrumbs are better than nothing.

I'm confronted by the classic intelligence dilemma: here are the things we think we know but are they fact or fiction, and even if they are accurate, what do they mean. and how should we, or in this case, I, respond?

"Harry, are you listening, or have you gone to that faraway place you go to hide?"

"I'm listening. I'm just debating in my mind how full of shit you really are."

"Not nice Harry, not nice at all, but I guess I deserve that?"

"Are you H. K. Krysa?"

"NO!"

The response comes too quickly and with too much force. Her denial only serves to make me more suspicious.

"Is that what the Commander told you, that I am the Beautiful Rat?"

"So you know."

"Yes, of course, I know. You are a smart boy Harry, but you do come to the game late, despite working hard to catch up."

"So why don't you catch me up now, before I throw you out of my car."

She looks at me strangely. She senses I'm serious and not just bluffing. "Okay Harry, you earned it. I suppose you need to know what this is really all about."

I pull over to the side of the road and park. I turn in my seat to face her. "You have my full and undivided attention."

She sighs one of her deliciously sensual sighs; she just can't help being sexy.

"Elections Harry, it's all about elections." She pauses allowing the significance of her words to sink in.

She continues, "The Russians screwed with the US election and the Brexit referendum, amongst a host of other similar attacks on Western democracies."

"Come on Harriet, that's very old news."

"Be patient, Harry... Their operations were successful, but of course, they ended with a shitstorm of consequences. But our Comrade pals are nothing if not inventive; a few conspiracy convictions in absentia aren't going to stand in their way of the next round of meddling. They adapt, adjust, and test, and Canada is ground zero for that testing.

The Sister Project's mandate is cyber disruption: create political chaos, social unrest, economic confusion, and stock market volatility. The people on our list are the ones in charge of the Canadian operation. Other similar groups are forming in the US, Great Britain, and throughout Western Europe. My job... our job, is to stop them, or at least slow them down."

"You mean Chester and Roger both work for the Russians?"

"They did. Everything is compartmentalized for security's sake. It seems Chester got a conscience and spilled the beans to Roger, but he didn't know Roger was on the list. That's what got him killed."

"So Roger killed Chester, not you?"

"More likely, had him killed."

"So who's H. K. Krysa?"

"I don't know, but that's what we need to find out."

"What about the other names on the list?"

"I guess you haven't heard the news. Tommy Harrison was killed in a hit and run this morning."

"Maybe they're cleaning house? Chester must have spilled his guts to his American bosses who told him to alert the Brits in an effort to flush out the other cell members. Poor Chester became expendable as soon as he told his bosses what he was involved in. Now Kyrsa is cleaning up the compromised group."

That's the last thing I remember before waking up on my couch in my apartment with a stiff neck and a sore back. On the coffee table were two Tylenol tablets, a glass of water, and a note from Harriet.

"I'm sorry Harry, I had to leave, but I was able to get you home after the incident. I didn't see who sideswiped us and I didn't call the cops. I sent your car to your mechanic, but it doesn't look good, I'm afraid the poor dear is on life supports. I'll be in touch. Love H"

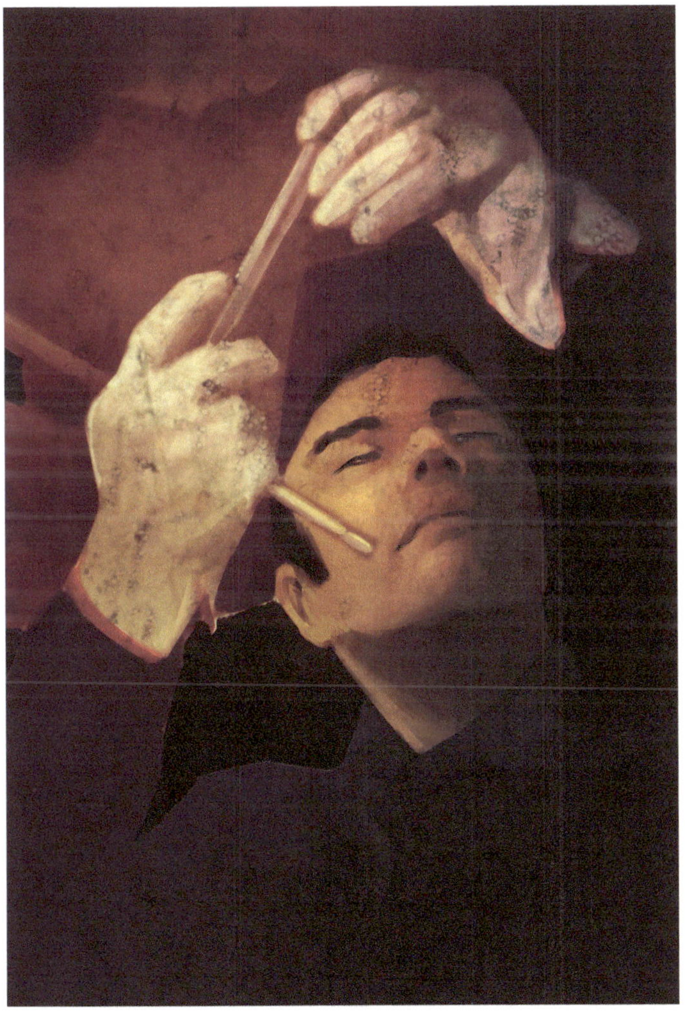

THE MECHANIC

The Mechanic

I stood in the Laoshu Garage looking at my poor damaged baby. Freddy Laoshu, my mechanic, specializes in British sports cars, a fondness he acquired in his youth, causing trouble on the streets of Hong Kong. He approaches. He puts his hand on my shoulder, "I'll make some calls to see if anybody has parts. As far as cost goes, I assume anything within reason."

I nod in agreement, too choked up to speak. Freddy senses my depression, "I'll do my best to resurrect the old dear, I know how much that car means to you. Just don't get your hopes up."

"I'll need some transportation in the meantime. What have you got?"

Freddy didn't hesitate, "What about that Karmann Ghia you had your eyes on. I, fixed the broken headlight last night. It's still got a few dents and scrapes but's it's mostly cosmetic; mechanically it's in great shape. The other stuff can be fixed anytime. I'll just need a few days."

"Sounds good Freddy, I'll take the Karmann Ghia. Why don't you fix the dents and give it a new paint job, but not red, too flashy for me. Make it black. Even if you can fix the MG, maybe it's time to keep the old girl for special occasions. Give me a call when it's ready and let me know how much I owe you."

"Tell you what... why don't you take my Healey in the meantime, maybe I can convince you to take both cars."

"You sure Freddy, I thought you'd never part with that car."

"The nice thing about being a mechanic is you can turn any old junker into a shiny new ride. It just takes the right amount of tender loving care."

As I drive out of Freddy's garage, I spot Harriet waiting for me across the street under a new billboard being installed. It seems the omnipresent advertising queen cornered the billboard market along with just about every other advertising medium.

I stop and roll down the window, "Need a ride?" She doesn't answer. She slides into the passenger-side bucket seat with the grace of a Serengeti cat. Watching her move is like licking the icing off the beaters of a gourmet's MixMaster; I had to stop myself from drooling. My epicurean-sexual fantasy is interrupted by Harriet handing me a slip of paper. It's a downtown address.

"What's at 57 Balfour Park?"

"Walter T. Marsh, right-wing conservative bagman for any pro-business, authoritarian asshole with deep pockets."

"I thought he was working for the Russians?"

"He'll take anybody's money if they put enough of it on the table, besides, the operation is probably being fronted and financed by one of the Russian oligarchs with ties to the SVR. Probably a buddy of the great man, himself."

"You think Kyrsa might be the oligarch?"

"No… that's too hands-on. Everybody needs deniability, at least, everybody important."

"I guess Tommy Harrison wasn't deemed important enough."

Harriet agreed, "I guess. Just a hacker for hire. An expendable cog in the wheel, like poor old Chester."

IN FOR A PENNY

"So maybe we use his vulnerability to turn him and get someone on the inside."

"It may be too late. With Chester and Harrison in the ground, they may be tying up loose ends by wrapping everything and everybody up..."

"Yeah, in body bags."

It turns out 57 Balfour Park is just around the corner from the Consulate General Of The Russian Federation. I park and open the driver's side door, Harriet doesn't move. "Aren't you coming?"

"No point in exposing both of us. You can fill me in when you get back."

I hesitated. What she said made sense: Harriet has been very careful, avoiding contact with anybody but me, at least as far as I know. There wasn't any point in both of us pouncing on Marsh.

On the other hand, maybe I was being offered up as the sacrificial lamb; an expendable Pawn offered as bait, so the Queen can make the final checkmate move.

She could see the wheels in my rusty brain grinding ever so slowly. She tries to reassure me "I'm not setting you up, Harry. Really, I'm not. You and I are partners... aren't we?"

I give her a fractured smile and nod understanding, despite the fact I feel like I've just been suckered again. *In for a penny...* as the saying goes, so off I go to the offices of Walter T. Marsh, political bagman, and Russian asset.

THE BAGMAN

The Bagman

As I enter the offices of Walter T. Marsh, I notice several young women and men frantically boxing files accompanied by the sound of shredders feverishly destroying what I assume is incriminating evidence of *Sister Project* activities. No one pays much attention to me. An attractive brunette balanced on her knees jams files into an already too full banker's box. She looks up at me.

"Where's Marsh?"

Her look says, please get me out of this madhouse. I offer no reprieve. "Marsh, where the hell is he?" My tone is harsh and demanding.

Her eyes plead for escape, to be fired or sent out for coffee and donuts and never to return. Anything to be released from this obvious den of extralegal activity. She points to an open walnut door with Walter T. Marsh, Financial Consultant painted in Engravers MT gold.

I pick my way through the confusion of boxes, scared temps, and soon to be fired secretaries. I enter Marsh's office. He's busy jamming papers into a shredder.

He notices my presence without bothering to look up, "Ask for Karen… she'll tell you what to run through the shredders and what to keep." He continues ramming things into the shredder finally jamming the damn thing. "Fuck!" He looks up at me with desperation in his eyes as if I was there to help.

I look him right in the eye, "You think Karen can point me to evidence of you working for the Russians?"

"What?"

"Stop shredding those papers."

"I can't, the machine's jammed…"

I turn around to face his staff, "Everybody! Stop what you're doing! STOP RIGHT NOW!" The room goes silent. They all stop. "I want everyone to line up over there." I point to the far wall. They all do as they are told.

I haven't shown a badge, search warrant, or any other official paperwork authorizing me to order anybody to do anything, but if you establish authority immediately, you can get away with almost anything, especially if your target is afraid they're in over their heads, like a room full of low paid office workers shredding evidence of espionage and election tampering.

"Which one of you is Karen?"

The young woman who directed me to Marsh's private office tentatively raises her hand. "Lock the front door. Don't allow anybody to leave."

I turn to face the group. "You are all under suspicion of disloyalty to the Government, under the Crime and Disorder Act of 1998. If you are found guilty of violating this act, you can be sentenced to life in prison.

Karen... make a list of everyone here, along with photocopies of their Social Insurance Numbers and Driver's Licenses. I suggest you cooperate. It will be considered when the time comes for you to be sentenced."

I was laying on the bullshit thick and fast before anyone could figure out I was bluffing. The Crime and Disorder Act is British law and since I was in Canada, it didn't mean shit, but they didn't know that. At this point, fear and intimidation are my greatest assets.

I point to a small box, "Karen, put all the SI numbers and driver's licenses in that box, along with everyone's cell phone."

That set off a rumble of grumbling from the assembled group, "I'd be more worried about who your cellmate will be in federal prison than I would about losing your cell phones... especially if it contains evidence of your direct involvement in your boss's espionage activities."

The threat of prison and a randy cell mate seemed to quiet the grumbling. "Everybody, sit on the floor and keep your mouths shut!"

I turn to Karen, "You know what to do?" She nods and goes to work collecting phones and wallets. I turn my attention to Marsh who is staring helplessly at the jammed shredder. He looks up from the stalled machine. "Listen... you got to help me. I think they're going to kill me, I need your protection."

"Not so fast, I need information on exactly what your *Sister Project* pals are doing, and I need the whereabout of H. K. Krysa. Then we can talk about protection."

Marsh had the look of a man who's headed for the gallows. He's defeated, and he knows it. "The information is in the safe."

"Where is it?"

"Behind the painting."

A painting of a character from what looked like a Wagnerian opera hung on the wall behind his desk over a credenza.

Wagner seemed appropriate for a right-wing asshole like Marsh. He started to head for the painting, "Don't touch it. in fact, don't fucking move."

I turn to look into the outer office. People are getting restless. Karen is texting someone on her cell phone. "What the hell are you doing?" I take three steps into the outer office and grab the phone out of her hand. I was too late, the message was already sent. It was simple, clear, and direct: *SEND THE CLEANERS!*

I went to the front door and unlocked it. "Everybody out." They went to retrieve their phones and wallets, "Don't touch that stuff. Get out while you still can." They hesitate. "Now... Move!"

I open the door and they scramble as fast as they can, stumbling over one another. Karen tries to leave, but I stop her. "No, you don't. Get the fuck in there." I point to Marsh's inner office. The three of us all stand looking at one another. I turn to Karen, "Do you know the combination to the safe?" She nods.

"Open it."

Marsh helps Karen take the painting off the wall, placing it on the floor beside the desk. I'm amazed I'm getting away with this charade of authority. I didn't have any right to do what I was doing, and I wasn't even pointing a gun at them.

Karen opens the safe with practised ease. She'd done it before and was obviously a bigger part of the operation than I initially thought. The safe contains stacks of neatly organized cash. Karen starts dumping the money on Marsh's desk.

She reaches back into the safe to retrieve something. She turns aiming a Nano 9mm pistol at my chest. She fires. I dive for the floor. My head hits the leg of a wooden office chair. Everything goes dark.

I couldn't have been out for very long. I hear arguing, a scuffle, and two more shots. I gather what's left of my senses and struggle to my feet. The money on the desk is gone. I spot Marsh's expensively tailored legs and nicely polished Florsheims sticking out from behind the desk. I look. He's dead. One bullet in the head and another in the chest. I smell smoke. I stumble into the outer office.

The box with all the SI numbers, wallets and cell phones is engulfed in flames. The bitch also set the rug on fire. I stumbled out the door and head for the stairs just as the sprinklers came on. I make my way down the stairs to the street with the sound of fire engines quickly approaching.

I have to get back to the car. I need Harriet's advice. I'm not in good shape, so it takes me a while to get there. I arrive back at the Healey with a migraine headache, a sore back, and a hole in my sports jacket where Karen's hastily aimed shot just managed to graze my arm. I get in the car, but Harriet is gone. Our suspects are slowly being eliminated. I flip open the glove box to see if Freddy kept some Aspirin handy. There are no pain pills, just a semi-automatic Beretta.

I assume Wade Gordon, the nutcase, talk radio host, and blogger must be next on Kyrsa's list. I stop to gather my thoughts. Is the pretty brunette, Karen, actually H. K. Kyrsa? If she is, it's genius, hiding in plain sight as a lowly administrative assistant, fucking brilliant. On the other hand, she might just be Marsh's assistant who realized the jig was up and decided to grab the money and run. What a mess.

This operation isn't limited to the names on the *Sister Project* list. Does Canada's cybersecurity agency, CSE, have any idea what the hell is going on? Do they, or the Russians, have eyes on me? I'm I on Kyrsa's to-do list? My head is spinning.

I start the car and head for Gordon's radio station where he is about to start his daily anarchist rant.

THE CONSPIRACY THEORIST

The Conspiracy Theorist

I arrive too late. The entire block is cordoned off by yellow crime scene tape. A body is covered in a sheet with dark red ooze creeping out from the edges where Gordon's head went splat. Police investigators scurry about collecting evidence and interviewing witnesses.

A crowd has gathered along with the usual gaggle of local news parasites interviewing anybody with a desire to get on the evening news. I overhear one reporter interviewing a female bystander that thinks she saw Gordon being pushed off the roof by a small blurry figure in black, but it could have just been his shadow. The silhouette was mostly hidden from sight by the roof-top billboard of the ever-present pitch girl. If the witness hadn't looked up at the billboard, she would have missed the whole thing. Lucky girl.

I feel a presence behind me. It's Harriet. She's changed her clothes. She's dressed in skintight black leather *à la* Emma Peel. She motions me to follow her back to my car. "Harry dear, you do look a mess."

I'm too sore and tired for our usual sexual banter, "Marsh is dead."

"Yes, I know. The lovely assistant, Karen, did the deed and took off with the cash. It appears, she almost did you in as well."

"How do you…" She stops me in mid-sentence "Come now Harry, I know everything you know. Don't you realize that by now? We are two peas in a pod. Remember?"

"You think Karen is H. K. Kyrsa? Maybe the 'K' stands for Karen."

"Harry dear, Karen is just Karen. Yes, she was Marsh's corrupted righthand and a greedy bitch, but she knew nothing about the Russian business. However, she did know about the cash in the safe and the gun. So when you exploded on the scene with your bad cop act, she figured, fuck-it, grab the money and run."

WHO'S PLAYING WHO?

Who's Playing Who?

It's time I confront Roger and find out which side he's on. I've been played by the Top Floor ever since I filed my report three months ago. I'm a pawn in some international chess game; set adrift in a quagmire of duplicity and intrigue and pronounced slightly unstable. That was the plan all along. They needed a patsy, and I was the perfect choice.

After all, I do tend to color outside the lines in my analysis, and besides. I'm only half British, not really one of them. The whole scheme is designed to give the brass plausible deniability.

I turn and look at Harriet, my god she is beautiful, but who the hell is she?

She turns up out of nowhere and plays me like a Stradivarius. I'm a fool. I fell for the whole goddamn deal, lock, stock, and smoking honey trap. I asked for a field agent and they pretended to blow me off, but secretly I'm the agent, the sacrificial lamb, and Harriet is running me.

The more I think of the deception, the angrier I get. I'm driving too fast. Harriet turns to look at me, "Calm yourself, Harry. We'll get to the bottom of this riddle."

I force myself to settle down. I have to maintain a clear head. They want me to act crazy, impulsive, and irrational. I need to fight the urge to scream.

I slow the Healey down and pull over to the side of the road. "Get out." The words come out of my mouth without me even knowing I said them.

"Okay Harry, I'll get out. I understand you're upset, it's natural, you just saw two people get killed. That's enough to push anyone over the edge."

And there it is, the setup, *poor old Harry, couldn't take the pressure. The Top Floor could see it coming. Tried to get him help, but he was too far gone. His imagination got the best of him, pushed him over the edge, went running in all directions. We just couldn't have that, something had to be done, the problem had to be eliminated. It's tragic really, more sad than anything, poor Harry...*

Harriet takes my hand in hers, bringing me back from that dark place I was headed. "Come back to me Harry. You can't afford to let your mental abstract expressionism get the best of you." Her words are soothing, almost sweet in their concern. I wanted to believe she meant it.

"Be careful Harry. Our movie isn't finished just yet; it isn't over till they run the credits." She leans over and kisses me on the cheek. She gets out of the car and heads down the street. I watch the black leather make its way down the block, she turns and smiles her delicious smile and disappears around the corner.

I'm angry but calm, almost too calm; it frightens me. I flip open the glove compartment and stare at the Beretta semi-automatic left there by Freddy.

Was it left there on purpose? Why does a mechanic have a gun in his car? Is Freddy part of the setup? Is Freddy, H. K. Kyrsa?

It doesn't make sense. He's Chinese from Hong Kong, not Russia. To hear him talk, he has little fondness for the mainland comrades. He left for Canada with his love for British sports cars before the big brother crowd took complete control.

The Karmann Ghia he's fixing... it's a German sports car, like the one the newspapers said killed Tommy Harrison. That would be perfect, me driving around in the murder weapon.

It doesn't matter; I take the gun out and check to see if it's loaded, it is. I put it in my jacket pocket. Roger may need some convincing to come clean. I put the Healey in gear and head for Roger's office.

When I arrive, I park under the billboard of the oppressively visible advertising beauty. I get out of the Healey on the street side.

I reach into my sports jacket to make sure my new Italian friend hasn't wandered off, leaving me defenceless. As I do, the familiar green Mustang wheels around the corner. The bastard from the Rosedale episode must have a mechanic too. I wonder if it's Freddy? Freddy and I are going to have a serious conversation.

The side window of the Mustang rolls down. I catch a glimpse of a stocking masked passenger aiming what could be a Glock 19 Machine Pistol in my direction.

My hand is still on the Beretta in my pocket. I pull the trigger. My sports jacket pocket explodes in protest. I fire again, and one more time for good luck.

I must have hit something despite the fact I didn't aim. because the American muscle car swerves out of control, climbs the sidewalk, and takes out a red Toronto Sun newspaper box. I never did think much of that right-wing tabloid. Funny, the things you think about when someone just tried to kill you.

The Mustang recovers with some added paint and styling contours left by the impact with the red newsstand box. He races off, escaping the area, obviously in fear of my untutored marksmanship.

I look down at my jacket. It too has been restyled by the encounter. It doesn't matter, the jacket was already ruined by Karen's attempt to cancel my ticket.

THE CONFRONTATION

The Confrontation

My instinct is to barge right into Roger's office and cause a fuss, but that will play directly into their scenario of crazy Harry going off the deep end. so instead, I wait in his outer office until I am summoned.

When the time arrives I act calm, but inside, a rage is building. I've been betrayed and somebody is going to pay. I will not be the patsy for the Top Floor or the Russians. This shell game has to be brought to a conclusion.

"Well, hello dear boy... Didn't know we had an appointment for today?"

"We don't." My answer is flat, unemotional, bordering on accusatory.

"You seem upset. I can see you must have been through some kind of nasty business. I'm afraid that nice sports coat of yours is beyond mending."

Roger is sitting behind his desk making notes in the margin of a report with his overly expensive Graf von Faber-Castell fountain pen; he waves the damn thing in my face like a symphony conductor demanding *pianissimo* from his musicians. "Sit, dear boy, sit."

I grab the pen out of his hand. "Don't patronize me, you pompous ass…"

"Sit down, Harry. Let's talk about it."

I regain my composure and sit in my usual chair. "I need you to be straight because I'm not playing your game any longer."

"I can see that dear boy. That Beretta you're holding tells me you mean business."

I didn't realize I was still holding the gun. I look at it as if it appeared on its own. I put the gun in the one pocket I have left.

"Can you be straight with me, Roger? I mean really straight, or are you here to just fuck with my head?"

"Harry, I'm on your side, whether you realize it or not. I know the Top Floor can be a bit inscrutable at times, but really, everyone just wants to get you back on track. Get all this fanciful imaginary nonsense behind you."

"Bullshit!" I pause gathering my thoughts.

"You know, that's the second time someone called my work 'fanciful.' The Chairman used that exact word when he dismissed months of work like it was a text message cancelling dinner. Odd you'd use that word. Someone might think you and the Chairman have an agenda, a playbook for setting me up to take the fall for this *Sister Project* business."

"Harry, old boy, you really do sound paranoid. Fanciful is a perfectly good word, meaning existing only in one's imagination."

"It may be a goddamn good word, Roger, but it sure sounds more like the usage of a sycophantic toddy parroting his deceitful superiors pompous turn of phrase."

"You have a creative mind, Harry, but it does get the best of you at times."

"Tell me, Roger, are you the Beautiful Rat? Are you H. K. Kyrsa?

"Who is H. K. Kyrsa? I'm afraid I've never heard of him... or her."

"I don't believe you. You're on the list."

"And what list would that be?"

"The *Sister Project* list."

"Never heard of it."

"I don't believe you."

"Where did you get this so-called list?" I hesitate to answer. He notices.

"Was it Harriet, Harry, the pretty woman you met in a bar? I'd like to meet this Harriet. Why don't you bring her along, because Harry, I don't think she exists? I think she is, and you'll excuse the term, a fanciful construction of your overactive imagination."

I reach into my pants pocket and pull out the napkin with the sketch I made of Harriet. I slam it down on Roger's desk.

"There! That's Harriet! She exists and so does the list! I'm not crazy, Roger. Ask Bowley. He's the one that told me about the *Sister Project*?"

"Bowley? You mean Commander Bowley?"

"Yes, of course. How many SIS assets do you know named Bowley?"

"Harry, I know Bowley was your friend and mentor, but Commander Bowley died a year ago. And this drawing you made looks a lot like someone I recognize."

"See… even you know she exists."

Roger gets up and goes to the window. "Come over here, Harry. I want to show you something."

I get up and go to the window. My hand instinctively massages the Beretta resting in my jacket pocket.

"Take a look, Harry. Tell me what you see?"

"The street, parked cars, the offices and shops across the road. What I'm I supposed to be seeing?"

"Look up higher Harry. What's on the roof?"

I look up. "The billboard? The stupid advertising billboard with the pitch girl. She's everywhere." Roger hands me the napkin.

"Take a good look Harry, that's your Harriet. You're right, she's everywhere, in fact, she's become almost invisible in her universal visibility.

I'm afraid you've developed some kind of trans-
ference. You've created an imaginary friend, or in
your case, a fictitious field operative, the one you
wanted so badly, but were denied. The Chairman
refused your request, so you made her up as a
substitute. You're ill, Harry, you need help."

I feel like punching Roger in his smug, arrogant
face, but I stick the napkin back in my pocket and
leave.

When I get back to the Healey, I realize I'm still
holding Roger's two thousand dollar pen. "Fuck
him." I stick the pen in my shirt pocket and get in
the car.

If Roger isn't Kyrsa, who the hell is? There are
only two suspects left, Harriet and Freddie. I
don't want it to be Harriet, and besides, Roger
says she's just a figment of my imagination.

Maybe he's right, or maybe he's just following the
brass's lead. It's typical of policemen, even ones
with MI6 credentials; instead of following the
leads, they come to the conclusion than find evidence to support it. I start the car and head to
Freddy's. He better have a goddamn good answer
to where he got that Karmann Ghia and why he
was pushing me to take it off his hands.

THE BEAUTIFUL RAT

The Beautiful Rat

*"I cannot forecast to you the action of Russia. It is a **riddle, wrapped** in a **mystery**, inside an **enigma**; but perhaps there is a key. That key is Russian national interest." - Winston Churchill*

There is a key to this puzzle and H. K. Kyrsa is the one who holds it. If Freddy is Kyrsa, I intend to make him talk.

I arrive at the garage and park the Healey in the back lot, a graveyard for misshapen derelicts and past their prime has-beens salvaged for parts.

I enter through the back door, not wanting to be seen until I'm ready. I remove Freddy's Beretta from my pocket. I hold it loosely letting my arm hang casually at my side.

I scan the room. The green Mustang that tried to do-me-in twice is up on a hoist. The dents and paint from the red newspaper box are still visible. The freshly painted Karmann Ghia stands beside my newly repaired MG in the middle of the shop. Freddy may be a traitor and an all-around shit-head, but he did know how to fix cars.

Freddy stands at a table in the corner bandaging the arm of the mechanic that accompanied him in their last attempt at ending my interference into their election meddling scheme. I didn't know if Freddy was the driver or the shooter, but my hastily fired response did draw blood. A Beretta similar to the one in my hand sits on the table beside a first aid kit. I accidentally kick a metal gasoline can.

Freddy and his mechanic lookup. "Harry, my friend, I've got your MG all fixed up. Good as new, I was just about to call you."

"Weren't you going to get rid of the damaged green Mustang first?"

Freddy scratches the sporadic stubble on his chin. He smiles a sheepish smile. "What can I say, Harry, it was just a job, nothing personal."

"I don't know Freddy. You tried to kill me twice. I kind of take that personally. I thought we were friends."

"Don't be naïve Harry. People like us don't have friends. Anyway... here's the keys to the MG." He tosses them hard at my head as he dives for cover while his mechanic reaches for the Beretta on the table, but I'm ready for him.

This time I aim and fire, hitting the mechanic in the shoulder, spinning him around, as he grabs for the gun. I fire again. The slug hits him in the chest. He tumbles over backward falling dead as his head hits the hard concrete floor.

I turn to see Freddy lying on the other side of the shop floor. His head is bleeding from where it collided with a large metal toolbox. He's stunned.

I make my way over to Freddy as he attempts to sit up. I aim the Beretta at his chest. "So Freddy, you're H. K. Kyrsa." It's not a question.

"If you say so, Harry."

"Well, are you Kyrsa or not? There doesn't seem to be any point in lying: the Mustang, the German sports car, and I'm sure if I nose around a bit I'll find other stuff that will put you away forever."

"Are you sure about that Harry?"

"Just answer the fucking question, are you Kyrsa or just one of his flunkies?"

Freddy sighs one of those big sighs of exhaustion mixed with exasperation. "There is no Kyrsa, Harry, it just the McGuffin in your mental movie, the mechanical rabbit the greyhounds chase around and around, and never catch."

"Don't give me that bullshit Freddy. I already heard that '*Harry you're crazy*' crap from my own people, I don't have to listen to it from a Russian agent."

"You just don't get it, Harry. Sure, Kyrsa is old Cold War code for someone running a cell, but it's just a joke. I don't work for the Russians."

"What the hell do you mean a joke?"

"My last name, Loashu… it means old rat in Chinese."

"You work for the Chinese?"

"Nope! Try again, Harry."

"You better fucking tell me before I put a bullet in your head."

"What the hell, why not? You're not going to do shit to me. In fact, my bet is you'll be the one going to jail for the rest of your life. You're the patsy, Harry. They'll get you for running over Tommy Harrison, for operating the *Sister Project*, and for killing my mechanic. Probably not a smart move on your part to shoot the mechanic."

"So who do you work for?"

"The Americans, Harry. It's the Americans that are fucking with the Canadian election. The administration doesn't like Canada's new age Liberal Prime Minister. It makes the President look like an authoritarian asshole. They want everyone on our side to move right. The *Sister Project* is just a pilot program. Canada, Great Britain, and the rest of the Western alliance will all be pushed further to the right. So Harry my friend, you are royally fucked."

"One last question Freddy, did you mess with the brakes on the MG?"

"No Harry, the MG is perfect. Langley decided they preferred you in jail, so they can trot you out now and again, to say, '*see... we need to move to the right to protect ourselves from evil foreign agents like dear old Harry*.' Poor Harry, fucked again. So my friend, why don't you let me go and I'll give you a head start. We'll see how far you get before they catch up to you."

There is nothing else to be said. When Freddy finishes, I pull the trigger. I'll have to find a new mechanic. I retrieve the gasoline can I kicked earlier and spread its contents around, making sure Freddy, the mechanic, and the Karmann Ghia are evenly coated with flammable liquid.

I realize Roger's expensive pen is still in my pocket. I wipe down the prints and throw it on the floor away from the worse of the gasoline hoping it will survive. Fuck Roger, let him try to explain why his overpriced pen was found in the middle of a crime scene.

I wipe my prints from the Beretta and place it in Freddy's hand. The whole messy scene looks like a shootout between the mechanic and Freddy. The pen will hopefully point the cops to Roger as the cleanup man.

I check for the keys to the MG. They're in the ignition. I drive my car out the back door to the lot where it's safe. I toss a match onto the trail of gasoline and leave.

As I head down the street away from the inferno, I see someone familiar standing beside one of those glass-enclosed bus shelters with a large advertising poster on the side. I don't have to tell you who is in the advertising poster or who is standing beside it. I stop.

Harriet slips into the car with her usual seductive grace. God, she is beautiful. She turns, "Looks like there's a big fire in your mechanic's garage. He'll be very unhappy."

"I think Freddy is beyond caring at this point. So Harriet, tell me, are you real, or just a figment of my imagination?"

She laughs that intoxicating laugh. She leans over the gear shift, grabs my chin twisting my head towards her. She kisses me hard using her teeth as an exclamation mark. I can taste the small trickle of blood she left behind.

"Real enough for you Harry?"

I may be crazy, and I may end up in jail but in the meantime, I got Harriet, cause in my movie, I always get the girl.

THE END

NOT QUITE AN EPILOGUE

Not Quite An Epilogue

The movie is over, or so you think. You get up and start to leave because who other than anal film geeks actually watch the credits; I mean, do we really need to know who supplied the doughnuts and coffee, or the name of the guy that drove the star to his midnight rendezvous with a corn beef sandwich on double rye?

As you struggle to put on your coat and jostle your way up the aisle while trying to convince your significant other that tacos are a far better post-movie indulgence than whole wheat muffins, you hear the hero's voice and realize the movie isn't over. You stop and turn as several other moviegoers charge into you on their way to the bathroom because bladders weren't designed for two-and-a-half-hour films.

You just paid thirty bucks plus the cost of a babysitter, parking, and two orders of Kung Pao Shrimp and General Tao's Chicken, so you *ain't* leaving till the damn thing is really over. You're determined to get your money's worth, so you stand in the aisle watching as other patrons batter you with their coats and umbrellas because everybody knows, leaving the movie theatre prompts Mother Nature to fuck with your freshly coiffed hair. In other words, this is the epilogue...

You're probably wondering what happened to Harry after he drove off into the sunset with his imaginary friend, Harriet, but wait, maybe she's real, and the Top Floor was actually screwing with poor old Harry's head, because they needed a patsy, and that's just what guys in the big offices do.

People do like closure, but life isn't like that, is it? Sure you got your beginning, middle, and end, but real life gets all muddled and messy, and just isn't conducive to high concept movie themes and series arcs, so let's review.

Harry is set-up by his secret agent pals who place him first in line for the role of prize-winning *putz,* but Harry fools them and kills his designated assassin and fellow minion while framing Roger for the nasty deed by absentmindedly stealing his overly expensive fountain pen and leaving it at the crime scene. I realize you just read the book so you should know all this stuff but some people just don't pay attention.

Is Harriet real or just a bit of cerebral cortex gone wrong? Does Harry get away with killing Freddy and his fellow button man? Does Roger get blamed for the killings? Does Harry still have a job? Do the Americans continue their efforts to mess with the Canadian Federal election? The truth is, I have no idea; you're just going to have to wait for the sequel.

THE OUTLAW RIDER

Other Books by Jerry Bader:

The Beautiful Rat

The Outlaw Rider
"If you're not prepared to cheat,
you're not prepared to win."

Jesse James, the daughter of a deceased mob-connected rug salesman, becomes a jockey working for the *Hong Mian* triad in order to feed winners to State Senator Samuel Somersby. The Senator is responsible for approving California gaming licenses. To date, only Native CANGV casinos are allowed to have slots. California horse racing will die if they aren't allowed to add slot machines to their venues. Benson Yeung, Dragon Head of the *Hong Mian* triad, and his chief lieutenant, Johnny Luck, have a plan to force Somersby to approve their Native partner's demands for off-reservation gaming licenses. At the center of the plan is a unique white thoroughbred Spirit horse, prized by Native people, appropriately named Medicine Hat.

Dead End
There Are No Good Guys

It all started five years earlier with the murder of Peter Pretty Boy Chen, a low-level soldier for Benson Yeung's Hong Mian triad. Rumor had it that the Guan Yu statue that sat on the old man's desk, the symbol of his Dragon Head status as leader of the Hong Mian, was filled with priceless Pigeon Blood rubies, or at least that's what Peter Pretty Boy Chen thought. Whether he was right or wrong is a tale for another time and another place.

What's significant is, his desire to get his hands on those rubies led to his brains being splattered all over the wall of the Green Dragon Restaurant. Like all classic California mysteries the past is never forgotten or forgiven; it always comes back to raise its ugly head.

DEAD END

DEAD END

Fast forward five years. We first met Jesse James and her associates in *The Outlaw Rider*, when she was a young female jockey making a name for herself on the track and off under the guidance of her mentor, triad big shot, Johnny Luck. Jesse has moved up the Hong Mian ladder and has made herself a major triad player, but the past is never so far behind that it doesn't affect the present. And so *Dead End* begins.

Palermo
A Place To Die

The race took place in picturesque Palermo, Sicily, but this wasn't your typical horse race with rules designed to protect the horses, jockeys, and bettors; this was a Mafia sponsored street race: a blood sport free-for-all more suited for the Coliseum than the backstreets of the scenic Sicilian town. Race promoter, Santos Luzzato, nephew to Nicky The Mushroom Fungo, wanted in on his American Uncle's horse racing connections with the LA triads. The race leads to a series of decisions that end with a suspicious car accident that kills billionaire heiress and racehorse owner, Josephine Somersby Murphy, sister to the Governor of California, Samuel Somersby, a man with Presidential ambitions and ties to Johnny Luck, LA triad big shot.

Love, sex, murder, and racehorses create a toxic mix of intrigue and suspense that drives Luck's protégé, Jesse James, to Sicily, Argentina, England, and Switzerland in her pursuit of the truth. Who killed Josephine Murphy? Was it Luzzato, Nicky Fungo, Murphy's brother, the Governor, or was it someone closer to Jesse.

Palermo, a place to die.

PALERMO

Stone Cold
Between a Stone and a Hard Place

On the surface, Major William Stone (Retired) is merely a rich, English expatriate with a diverse military and financial services background now living in Palermo, Argentina where he runs a small art gallery along with his assistant Margarita Cervantes.

If you scratch the surface, you'll find that Stone was recently the chauffeur for Mrs. Josephine Murphy, heiress to the Murphy Peanut Butter Company, the largest peanut butter manufacturer in the USA, and owner of numerous expensive thoroughbred racehorses. This seemingly incongruous set of circumstances gets even more intriguing when you learn that Stone inherited over one billion dollars when Josephine Murphy died in a tragic, and somewhat questionable, car accident in the hills of Palermo, Sicily leaving Major Stone the bulk of her estate.

After the Murphy estate is settled, Stone disappears to reemerge in Argentina leading a quiet and peaceful life as a wealthy art gallery owner and financier. His good fortune is tempered by the fact he left the love of his life, Jesse James, protégé to gangster Johnny Luck, back in LA.

The problem is, Major William Stone died in the Falkland Islands and the man now assuming his modified identity is disgraced MI6 financial wizard Jacob Conrad. Conrad took the fall for his Vauxhall Cross masters' illegal shenanigans ending up in jail with a lengthy prison term. According to the British newspaper reports, Conrad died in Belmarsh Prison, only to be resurrected by Section Six's cyber boffins as William Stone, international financial consultant living in Hong Kong, where he runs into Charlie Long, Dragon Head of the Wan Chai and a major rival of the Hong Mian, led by Benson Yeung and Johnny Luck.

Stone Cold dives deep into the back-story of how Jacob Conrad becomes William Stone, why he disappeared leaving Jesse behind, and who'll control the flow of cocaine into the USA. From Hong Kong to Palermo, London, Cacaloxuchitl, Mexico and Los Angeles, this is a tale of secret agents, drug dealers, money launders, and murders, all wrapped in a delicious recipe of greed, envy, cocaine, and peanut butter chili.

The Aussie Switch
Published By MRPwebmedia

Horse trainers, Davey and Pauly Cisco are looking for a fresh start in Southern California after wearing out their welcome in their native Australia. The Cisco twins are identical in looks but not personality; Pauly, like most horse trainers, pushes the envelope of acceptable practice, while his look-alike brother rips through regulations with regularity and abandon. It didn't take long for the two brothers to hook-up with a couple of conmen: an expert computer hacker who likes e-gaming and a shyster stock promoter on the lookout for eager marks willing to blow their fortunes on a shady horse-betting consortium. The one thing they didn't count on is an associate of Benson Yeung's Hong Mian triad; an ex-South Korean Colonel who operates a crooked international gambling empire. Two corrupt confidence men, unethical twin horse trainers, and doppelgänger thoroughbreds add up to a combustible confluence of confusion, miss-direction, and murder, with tentacles that twist their way through LA, Sidney, Hong Kong, Seoul, and Macau.

STONE COLD

Ballet of Bullets
The Game Is Dodging Death
Published By MRPwebmedia

Internet gambling and the expansion of casinos beyond the Nevada State Line have put a financial strain on racetracks. Johnny Luck, Hong Mian triad big shot, and his beautiful blonde ex-jockey protege, Jesse James, are always on the lookout for ways to expand the triad's gambling operation. Back in the fifties and sixties, Jai Alai was a big deal in Florida. Gamblers would fill the *frontons* and drop thousands of dollars betting on Basque athletics competing in a sport that was so dangerous it was referred to as the Ballet of Bullets and The Game Is Dodging Death.

Johnny Luck sees the potential revenue that could be produced by resurrecting the all but dead blood sport. The question is, how to make it popular again? Jesse has the answer. Television. People will bet on anything; they will also watch anything, as witnessed by the plethora of cooking shows that feature ordinary people competing for who can fry the best egg.

If there's a competition, people will bet on who will win. But where there is money, there is corruption; enter the Miami Bettor's Club, run by old Hong Mian rivals Tommy The King Kong and Marco Antonia Suarez, nicknamed *El Astronauta*. In the end, the Ballet of Bullets becomes all too real for the people fighting for control of the gambling revenue generated by the International Jai Alai League.

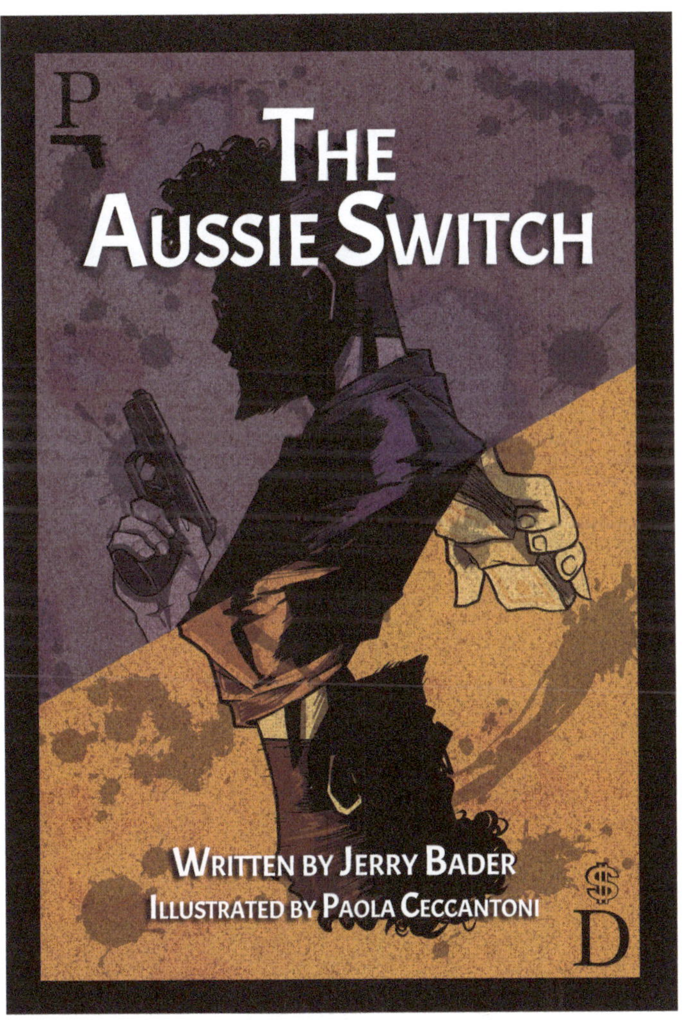

THE AUSSIE SWITCH

What's Your Poison?
How Cocktail's Got Their Names
Published By MRPwebmedia

Why do we call mixed alcohol drinks "cocktails"? How do they get their exotic names: names like the Singapore Sling, Screw Driver, the Alamagoozlum, the Angel's Kiss, the Hanky Panky, the Harvey Wallbanger, Sex On The Beach, the Monkey Gland, the Brass Monkey, the Margarita, the Japalac, the Lion's Tail, and many, many more? Who makes up these names, where are they invented, why, and how do you make them? These questions will be answered in *"What's Your Poison?"* by exploring the incidents, people, and places that prompted the creation of these exotic concoctions.

Organized Crime Queens
The Secret World of Female Gangsters

From the bizarre world of female Japanese motorcycle gangs to the historic rise and fall of London's Forty Elephants, the history of female organized crime is both fascinating and strange. These are the stories, both true and legendary of the female crime bosses that broke the mould of feminine gentility. This is The Secret World of Female Gangsters.

Cowboys, Lawmen, & Outlaws

When we think of the Old West, it seems like ancient history, but historically it was yesterday. Many of the characters of the post Civil War Old West lived well into the twentieth century: Bat Masterson died in 1921 and Wyatt Earp didn't pass-on until 1929. Josie Bassett, one of the Wild Bunch girls managed to hang-on until 1963 and she only died then because she got kicked in the head by a horse.

BALLET OF BULLETS

History doesn't end with an era, remnants, artifacts, and people overlap. History doesn't stop because technology and style move on.

The future is more likely to look like the film *Brazil* with its jury-rigged conglomeration of antique flotsam and modern-day technological jetsam, than the bright shiny newness of *Star Trek*. Turning history into fantasy is dangerous; it leads to mistaken notions and bad decisions. Maybe it's time to grow up and see the heroes of the Old West, as they really were, cowboys, lawmen, and outlaws.